P9-DNL-180

The Elixir Fixers

Sasha and Puck and the Potion of Luck

Daniel Nayeri

Illustrated by Anneliese Mak

Albert Whitman & Company
Chicago, Illinois

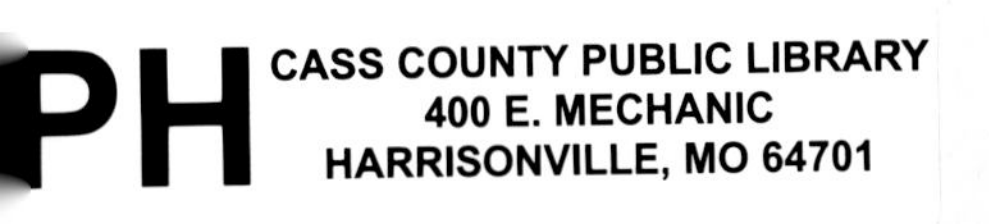

Library of Congress Cataloging-in-Publication data
is on file with the publisher.

First published in the United States of America
in 2019 by Albert Whitman & Company
ISBN 978-0-8075-7242-9

Printed in the United States of America
10 9 8 7 6 5 4 3 2 1 BP 22 21 20 19 18

Design by Ellen Kokontis

For more information about Albert Whitman & Company,
visit our website at www.albertwhitman.com.

To Adventure

MAP OF THE VILLAGE
SPARKSTONE MOUNTAINS
THE OLD TREE
A MYSTERIOUS PLACE
CATHEDRAL
SWEATING RIVER
CAKER
MAYOR'S HOUSE
GRANNY YENTA'S HOUSE
JEWELER
THISTLEWOOD SWAMP
SHIVERING RIVER
CENTRAL MARKET
GROCER
THE JUICY GIZZARD
MILLER
VILLAGE SQUARE
BAKER
COBBLER
DOCKS
INN
PAVLOV'S HOUSE
BLACKSMITH
STABLES
STONE LAKE
WHISPERSHAW CASTLE

CHAPTER 1

Sasha hid behind a display of glass bottles and held her breath. She made a bad spy. She was bad at being silent.

Her toes tapped. Her fingers wiggled with the desire to order the bottles just so. She groaned every time Papa made an unfunny joke to a customer of their alchemy shop.

Ms. Kozlow fussed with the clasp of her coin purse as she stood at the counter. She seemed very nervous, even though she was very elegant, thought Sasha, and must have been twenty years old at least.

Papa studied a muddy brew in a glass vial through his spectacles.

"Now, Mr. Bebbin," said Ms. Kozlow, "I don't want this...this—"

"Potion, madam," said Papa.

"Yes, potion. I don't want this potion to give me *too* much luck. I only need *just enough* luck."

"Of course, of course," said Papa as he grated a wrinkly, old mushroom into the drink.

Sasha ran out of breath. She let out a gust of air and inhaled another. She slapped her hand over her mouth, hoping they hadn't heard her in the far corner of the shop. She ducked down below the display of bottles filled with sleep sand and squatted next to a crate of bird eggs. She paused to make sure the giant stone phoenix egg hadn't crushed the tiny, speckled quail eggs.

Ms. Kozlow went on. "I've got a lovely little place in the Village, you see. And my bonbons are selling quite well. I wouldn't want too much luck to ruin it all. I could inherit some far-off castle, for example, and then I'd have to go clean out the moat every Thursday."

"Hmm," said Papa. He was focused on measuring the ingredients.

"Or imagine if I won some sort of contest to have a pet tiger. What would I do with a tiger in my chocolate shop?"

Sasha could think of about a thousand things one could do with a tiger in a chocolate shop. She wished she could list each one for Ms. Kozlow, but she was spying on their conversation, as she always did with the customers. That meant no interrupting. She let out a sigh instead.

"No, no," said Ms. Kozlow, "I need a *precise* amount of luck."

Sasha sighed again. She couldn't believe how many people in the Village believed in things like potions, magic, and alchemy—including her father, of course. It was all so...silly.

"It would help my calculations," said Papa, "if I knew what this precise amount of luck was for."

"Oh, *no, no, no,*" said Ms. Kozlow, bringing her purse up to her chest. "It's a private matter, I'm afraid."

Sasha noticed that Ms. K wore gloves. No one else in the Downside of the Village wore gloves. Sasha guessed she was either from Upside, or she didn't have the time to get all the chocolate out from under her nails.

"Very well," said Papa, stirring the liquid with a dried stalk of mandrake root. "Then I'll need to know your exact hair color."

"I'd say 60 percent dark-chocolate brown," said Ms. K, patting her crown of braids.

"I see," said Papa. "And do you prefer a hamster or a ham bone?"

Ms. K blinked a few times. "I suppose I prefer hamsters…but not to eat."

"Of course not," said Papa. "That would be a silly question. And when was the last time you ate a green apple?"

Ms. K thought for a moment. "Last Tuesday, at noon."

"Excellent." Papa plucked a yellow berry from a potted plant sitting on the far side of the counter and dropped it into the mixture. The potion fizzed up to the rim and made a *PLIP PLOP* sound. Papa seized the mandrake root and stirred the brew furiously until the liquid calmed back down. "All right then," he said. "Yes, I think so. This is *exactly* the amount for *just enough luck*." He plugged the glass vial with a cork and handed it to Ms. Kozlow.

"Why is it...that color?" asked Ms. Kozlow, wrinkling her nose.

Sasha thought it looked like swamp water.

"I could add some strawberry jam," said Papa.

"That would help the color and with the taste of dung beetle."

Ms. Kozlow held the potion bottle with two fingers as Papa looked around his messy shelves.

Finally, he turned around and said, "I've got good news and bad news. I found the jar of jam. Unfortunately, it's empty."

He held up the jar that Sasha had finished that morning.

Ms. Kozlow frowned. "What terrible luck. It looks like I came to you just in time." Ms. K gave Papa a few coins from her purse. Then she pulled out two chocolate bonbons and placed them on the counter. "One for you, and one for your daughter," she said. "Thank you, Mr. Bebbin. You've saved my life."

Papa blushed.

From behind the display shelf, Sasha wanted to shout, *Don't take it! Have some sense, woman! It's not safe!* There was no telling what someone would do if they thought they were magically lucky. What if Ms. K jumped off a barn thinking she might be lucky enough to land on a passing sheep?

The door swung shut behind the chocolate maker, and Sasha was about to stand up when a head suddenly appeared over her.

"You can come out now," Papa said as he wiped down the counter. "You need to get better at sneaking, if you're going to spy on our customers."

CHAPTER 2

Sasha sprang from her hiding spot, feeling a bit childish. She smoothed her tunic and straightened her shoulders. Another sale was another disaster waiting to happen. Sasha much preferred the customers who bought fancy eggs for decorating or milk from Cordelia, their dairy cow. Papa was a respectable apothecary and had a wondrous garden of strange plants that could help sick people get better. But whenever he used them for his crazy potions, Sasha was fear-stricken and furious at the same time.

Customers like Ms. K, who believed in all that hocus-pocus, were bound to be disappointed. Potions *didn't* work—at least, not Papa's potions. Sasha had a vague memory that her mother was the alchemist of the family, and maybe her potions had worked, but that was a long time ago. These days, it was Papa working from her mother's recipe books, and Sasha wasn't convinced. She was certain the magic was gone.

And soon, the few customers they had would complain. But Papa would insist that his calculations were correct. And then they would take Papa to the constable. And the constable would make Papa pay a huge fine for lying. And Papa wouldn't be able to pay it. *And then* she and Papa would go bankrupt. *And then* Vadim Gentry would buy up their store. *And then* they would be homeless. *And then* they would wander the countryside in poverty.

And when Mother returned from her long journey, she would never find them.

It had happened to a potion-maker in Sandtown last summer and in Rozny the year before. Papa needed to be more careful.

Sasha's heart was pounding with her runaway fears by the time she approached the counter. "Why did you promise her magic luck?"

"All luck is magic," said her father, as he poured the chalk dust he had used earlier into its porcelain container. "And I didn't promise it to her. That's simply what the potion *does*."

Sasha sighed and puffed her cheeks. She didn't have time to argue magic and science again. Ms. Kozlow would be walking back to the Village now, expecting some sort of extra-special luckiness.

"Of all the odds and oddity, *Papa*," she said in her most imposing voice, "chances are she won't

get whatever she wants, and then she'll blame you. You *must* go to Ms. Kozlow and take back the potion."

Her father was a kind man. Tall, thin, with a ring of brown hair around his bald head. He wore the thickest glasses Sasha had ever seen. His mustache had already gone white and would shake whenever he was trying to hold back a laugh.

Sasha added, "You can tell her the mandrake root was moldy."

Her father chuckled. "But moldy mandrake doesn't affect anything," he said.

"I know," she said.

"I know you know, darling."

"That's because the whole potion doesn't affect anything," she said.

"Ah. There, my sweet daughter, you are wrong."

Sasha sighed and moved on to plan B. These days, plan B was pretty much plan A. It was up to Sasha to make sure the potions worked—not magically, but scientifically. And to do that, she had to do some detective work. She grabbed her satchel of tools from behind the counter.

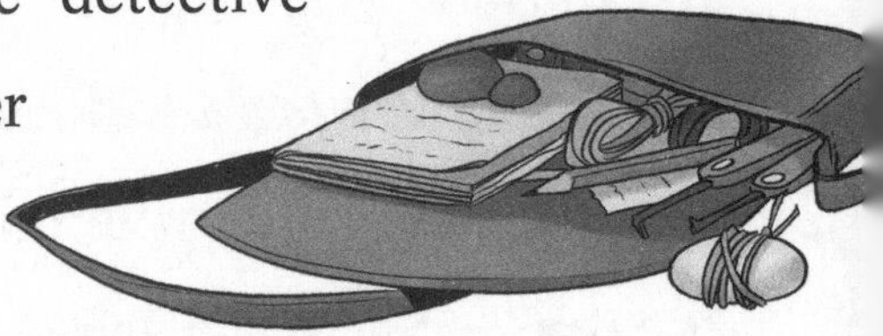

"Would you like me to make a batch for you?" asked her father. "Then you might have some luck convincing your father."

"Gregor says there's no such thing as magic

and there's no such thing as luck."

"Pah, Gregor is too narrow-minded. Scientists only know what other scientists tell them. You should be spending more time learning the family trade."

Sasha could hear him gearing up for a long speech. "Papa, this is serious."

"So am I! You're a lucky child! Having a loving father is lucky," he mused.

Sasha was ready to leave, but the countertop was still a mess of ingredients. As he walked around the shop putting bottles away, Sasha walked behind him, rearranging them into their proper places.

"Getting your mother's sharp mind," he added, "that's *very* lucky."

Sasha didn't mention that having a wandering alchemist for a mother was the unluckiest thing she could imagine. It would have sounded like she was blaming him. But in the silence, she realized they were both thinking it.

She looked at her papa, who was cleaning the oil burner and the hot plate that sat on top of it. He gave her an apologetic smile.

Sasha said, "Oh, Papa, why couldn't you give Ms. Kozlow some borgum root? Or peach tea? That would have lowered her blood pressure. People feel luckier when they're relaxed."

"That would be a trick," said her father.

"With better odds of working."

"Didn't you see her face?" said her father. "This was a case for magic."

Sasha turned to leave.

"Sasha Liliana Bebbin," said Papa.

She stopped.

She turned back.

"We have an agreement, the two of us, do we not?"

"Yes, Papa. We never leave each other angry."

She rushed over to hug him. She would never abandon him, she thought. And the truth was that Sasha had never *disproved* magic, and so, scientifically speaking, she had to make room for the possibility that it existed. Maybe there was real magic somewhere out in the world. But not in their boring valley. Magic didn't happen there.

Ms. Kozlow would be nearing the Village by now, and Sasha had to catch her.

"Here," said her father. "Ms. Kozlow left you a couple of bonbons."

Sasha knew that one of those chocolates had been for him. He was giving up his own treat for her. But she didn't want to refuse his kind gesture. She wrapped them in her handkerchief and put them in her satchel.

"You worry so much, Sasha."

"I really must go," she said.

But he didn't hear her. "Your mother would know what to say. She understood all this," he said, nodding at the alchemy lab. "Do you know she used to leave candies in the woods behind the shop?"

"What for?" said Sasha.

"For luck, of course."

"For Otto to find and devour, you mean," said Sasha. Otto was their family pig. A very stuck-up pig. A runt-sized pig, about as big as a loaf of bread, who ruled their yard like a goblin king. He was usually calm when he was well fed. But if anything crossed him—if he smelled griddle cakes or saw the color orange—then the whole Village trembled.

"No. They weren't for Otto. Even he won't go into the dark part of the forest. There are wood elves in there, don't you know? And little sprites who dance in the river with the *rusalkas*. If you listen on moon nights, you can hear their music—the children of Veles, the trickster, who makes luck. They loved your mother, you know. That's why they live so close. They grow the ether pearls we find in the riverbank. Sometimes, their tangled hair sprinkles pollen from fields beyond the fairy kingdom, and flowers come up in our forest that we haven't seen for two chapters of the world."

"Really?" said Sasha. "Mother left them food?"

"Every moon night."

"For luck?"

"For luck. For you."

Sasha thought about it for a moment. If there *were* any sprites in the woods, they had yet to hold up their part of the bargain with her mother. And, scientifically speaking, that made them liars. Sasha looked out the window and wondered if they would ever see her mother walking back down the lane.

"Not everything can be explained," her father was saying.

"Uh, Papa?" said Sasha, sitting up suddenly to get a better look out the window.

"What is luck, anyway—"

"Father!"

"Yes? What is it?"

"Ms. Kozlow didn't leave. She's outside."

Sasha pointed at the young chocolatier, who had seen their newborn chickens in the coop.

"She's just petting the chicks," said Papa, adjusting his glasses. Ms. Kozlow was bending over to offer the babies gentle rubs on their heads.

"Yes," said Sasha, "but look at what she's wearing!"

"Uh-oh," said Papa. "That's unlucky."

Sasha ran out of the shop as quickly as she could, hoping to catch Ms. Kozlow before Otto caught sight of her bright-orange skirt.

Crumbsy bumsy, thought Sasha as she jumped down the stairs of the alchemy shop and onto the dirt lane.

Ms. Kozlow was still bent over, petting chickens.

She didn't notice Otto at all.

The little pig was ten feet away. He had already spotted her orange skirt. He was stamping his hooves in rage.

"Look out!" shouted Sasha.

But it was too late.

Otto charged.

Sasha sprinted.

"Look out! Look out!"

Otto was almost there.

This is going to hurt, thought Sasha.

BAM!

Sasha tackled the pig just as he was about to ram into Ms. K.

They fell into the yard and scared all the chickens.

Ms. Kozlow finally noticed. When she saw Sasha and Otto smash into each other, she said, "Oh my!"

Sasha's head spun. She held on to Otto with all her might. The little pig kicked and snorted and still wanted to attack Ms. K.

Ms. K had no idea, of course.

"What's this?" she said. "A game?"

"Nnnnnoooooo," said Sasha, her jaw rattling.

"Oh," said Ms. K. "Is this pig bothering you? Should I get the constable?"

"Nnnoo help. My bag. Get my bag," said Sasha. Otto wiggled and bucked while Ms. K grabbed Sasha's satchel from the dirt.

"OK," she said, "should I hit him with it?"

That would only anger Otto more.

"No!" said Sasha. "The bonbons. Give him the bonbons."

Her arms were so tired she could hardly feel

them.

Ms. K said, “But these are 72 percent Teluvian chocolate with wildberry cordial filling. We couldn’t give them to a…a pig.”

“Now!” said Sasha. “If you want to live!”

She had to let go. He was too slippery. And he kicked harder than a mule. How could such a little creature have such powerful wiggles?

As soon as Sasha let go, Otto charged at Ms. K.

She let out a yelp and dropped the bonbons.

Otto stopped short when he saw the chocolates. He gobbled them up.

He loved chocolate.

Sasha breathed a sigh of relief.

“That was close,” she said.

Ms. K stared at Otto as he wandered back to his mud pit, happy now that his belly was full.

“It was your skirt,” said Sasha. “Otto sees red when he sees orange.”

"What a terrible coincidence," said Ms. K, "that I wore my orange skirt today, of all days."

"Yes," said Sasha, "but it was very lucky that I looked out the window when I did, wouldn't you say?"

"Hmm?" said Ms. K. She was still a little in shock.

"Wouldn't you say you've had good luck overall?"

"Oh, yes," said Ms. K.

"The potion must be working already," said Sasha.

"That can't be," said Ms. K. "I haven't had a sip yet."

She pulled the bottle from her skirt pocket and held it up.

Crumbsy bumsy! Sasha thought, as she picked herself up and patted the dirt from her legs.

"Maybe the top was loose," said Sasha, "and

a little of the potion rubbed off on your fingers."

It wasn't a very believable story.

Ms. K said, "Perhaps."

Sasha hurried to think of some excuse to follow Ms. Kozlow back to her shop, but she was interrupted.

"Sasha, would you come with me to my shop?"

What luck! thought Sasha. Of course, she didn't believe in luck, only in the mathematical potential for various outcomes. She believed any good scientist would look at a situation and weigh the likeliness, or odds, of each outcome. Then she would pick the one with the best chance of coming true. So she amended her thought: *What probability!*

"Sasha?" said Ms. Kozlow.

"Oh. Yes, sorry. I was just thinking something."

"I was saying if you come to my shop, I could thank you again and replace the bonbons."

"You're very kind," said Sasha.

And so, the two began to walk along the lane, down the hill, toward the Village.

As long as Sasha had been alive, and a lot longer before that, people just called the village, "the Village."

It didn't have a name, because it wasn't a famous place, like the Knight Garden, or the Citadel of the Make Mad Order, or even Rozny,

the town on the other side of the mountains.

Everyone who knew about the Village lived there. And anyone who didn't live there didn't know about it. So it had never needed a name.

The Village sat in a meadow in a little valley beyond the Willow Woods, between two rivers that flowed into each other and out into the King of Seas. In the mornings, the fog from the sea would roll over the Village, into the woods,

and make it a dreamlike place where people would see magical creatures of all kinds. Sasha only saw people and trees and everyday stuff.

The valley with the Village was just a little place compared to the rest of the world. It was tucked away in an out-of-the-way corner, where no kings or wizards ever took notice. And the war was just a far-off rumor. News from the wider world reached them when travelers passed through or when the musicians guild in Rozny graduated a new class of bards and they all set out on their first adventures over the Sparkstone Mountains.

Sasha knew all the stories about hill trolls and castles where the flowers could talk. She knew the war effort had called all the dragon riders and alchemists. That's where her mother had gone—to heal the wounded and the sick. And maybe some of it was magic. To be honest, Sasha couldn't remember that part.

Sasha had never been to Rozny or to anywhere else. The Village was the only home she'd ever had. Which was why it was so important to make sure they never lost the shop. Which was why she had to make sure Ms. K got her luck.

As they walked, Sasha noticed that Ms. K had a nervous habit of humming to herself. Sasha didn't recognize the tune.

"Do you like being a chocolate maker?" asked Sasha. *Maybe Ms. K needed luck to find a new job.*

"Oh, I adore it," she said. "All five of my aunts were chocolatiers."

Nope.

"Is it hard?" said Sasha. Maybe she needed luck to make some particular bonbon.

"It's hard to get cacao here in the valley," said Ms. Kozlow, "but when the caravans pass through, I stock up as much as I can."

Sasha wasn't getting anywhere. They passed the wooden signpost that said:

THISTLEWOOD SWAMP, THIS WAY.

WILLOW WOODS, THAT WAY.

THE KING OF SEAS, THAT OTHER WAY

VILLAGE, AHEAD.

The dirt lane turned into a cobblestone path. The first building was the miller's house, sitting beside the stone bridge, where the water wheel turned in the lazy river.

They passed a half dozen houses, the Wander Inn, and Moxley's Tavern.

Sasha peppered Ms. K with questions.

Was she happy in the Village?

Yes.

Was she going to be in a bonbon competition anytime soon?

No.

Did she want to be rich?

Not really.

Was she in love?

Nervous laugh. No answer.

Did she have a mom and dad?

Yes, both.

That was already very lucky, said Sasha.

“Yes,” said Ms. K, “but mine aren’t very much like yours.”

Sasha didn’t want to ask any questions about mothers. They walked through the Village square where the greengrocer, the cheesemonger, the baker, and the spicer all had a little market together. The bigger market with the goldsmith and the jeweler was in the part of the Village people called “Upside,” where the wealthy families lived. Two

rivers cut across the Village: the warm Sweltering River that flowed from deep within the Willow Woods, and the cold Shivering River that rushed from high up in the mountains. The fancy Upside neighborhood was upriver on both rivers. The Gentrys lived there.

The rest of the Village, the square and its markets, were in Downside, where most of the working people lived. It was downriver, of course.

The docks by the sea, where the butcher and tanner worked, were called "Dockside," and Sasha wasn't allowed to go there alone.

"I'm sorry," said Ms. K. "I see I've upset you."

Sasha wiped her eyes. "No," she said.

"I only meant that your father seems to love you very much. He smiles often."

"That's true," said Sasha.

"And does he support your desire to be a detective?"

"Detective?" said Sasha. "What makes you think I want to be a detective?"

"Oh," said Ms. K. "I just thought that since you had your notepad and were asking questions..."

"I'm not sure what I want to be. I'm only twelve."

"Okay," said Ms. K.

"But Papa is very supportive of me."

"That's all I meant," said Ms. K.

That was close, thought Sasha. Obviously, she wanted to be a detective, but a good detective wouldn't want the people she's detecting to know they were being detected. So she put Ms. K off the scent. And besides, Sasha wanted to detect the world and all its secrets—all the hidden laws of science.

She didn't have time to explain science detection. They had already come to the street where Ms. K lived. It was just over the bridge, on the Upside of the Village.

"Your dad doesn't smile often?" asked Sasha. That part had sounded important.

"Oh, never," said Ms. Kozlow. She stood up a bit straighter, as if her father had told her to fix her posture.

Ms. Kozlow's house was a thatched cottage at the end of a narrow street. A sign above the door read "Le Bon Bonbon" in swirly iron letters.

In the windows, Sasha could see a display of chocolate truffles—some lined up inside velvet jewelry boxes, others stacked in pyramids on glass trays. Ms. K had arranged orchids in between the various flavors and shapes.

"Wow," said Sasha.

"Thank you," said Ms. K. "We moved here last fall from Rozny."

"I've never seen anything like it."

"You should visit me, then. I feel like I've been talking to a sister."

"Thank you," said Sasha, but she couldn't take her eyes from the incredible assortment of chocolates in perfect, little squares. It all seemed very orderly. *Ms. K would make a good apothecary*, thought Sasha. She seemed very strict—like she would be unforgiving of potions that didn't work.

It did make Sasha think of one question. "You must be hoping to leave this back alley, no?"

"Why?"

"So more people can see your work. It's beautiful."

"Oh, thank you, but this little cottage is perfect. We don't get any sunlight, since we're tucked back behind these other buildings. It helps the bonbons stay nice and cool. And we can attract customers from both Upside and Downside."

Sasha couldn't help but sigh. Ms. Kozlow seemed like the luckiest woman in the world. What more could she want?

Inside, the shop was even more amazing. Everywhere Sasha turned, there was a tray of chocolate bonbons in rare and exotic flavors. Each shelf had color-coded flowers to indicate the fillings inside the chocolates. Red poppies lay beside chocolates filled with dragon pepper jelly. Yellow irises sat beside truffles dusted with sun fairy powder. Purple hibiscus blossoms stood beside bonbons drizzled with gooseberry cream.

"Pick any one you like," said Ms. Kozlow.

But all Sasha could think of was Ms. K reporting the potion to the constable.

"Ms. Kozlow," she said, "can I ask you something?"

"Of course," said Ms. K.

"Why would someone so beautiful and

talented, who lives in a flowery chocolate shop, need any luck at all?"

Ms. K blushed so red that all her freckles seemed to glow.

"Is it because your dad is very strict?"

Ms. Kozlow didn't say anything. She took a truffle from four different trays and wrapped them in a light tissue paper. She gave the bundle to Sasha with a half smile.

"Thank you again, Sasha," said Ms. K. She seemed to have gone cold. Sasha knew this was a polite way of saying the conversation was over.

"Okay," she said, "I hope you enjoy your potion and it brings you luck."

"Thank you."

"Because it will. I mean. They do. The potions. They work. They work very well. My father is a good man." Sasha ran out of the shop before she could make even more of a fool of herself. She walked around the side of the shop as fast as she could, so Ms. Kozlow couldn't see her. She leaned against the stone wall in the dark alley.

That was a complete mess, she thought. But what could she do? Ms. K wanted luck, and Sasha had to find out why.

Ms. Kozlow was very buttoned-up. Sasha would have to do her best spying. Could she wait here in the dark until Ms. K went out again? Could she follow and find out her secret reason for wanting luck?

Sasha's eyes weren't used to the shadows.

As she planned her next move, she started to notice a strange grunting noise behind her.

Suddenly, Sasha realized that she wasn't alone.

And whatever was there with her was right in front of her.

Sasha froze.

Her eyes slowly made out the shapes before her. A stack of crates stood on one side of the alley. At her feet was a pile of ash where a chimney sweep must have dumped the soot from all the nearby buildings.

Sasha wanted to turn and run. But she had heard that any sudden move might startle a creature and make it attack.

Sasha kept stone-still.

The grunting noise was coming from the soot pile. She reached out her foot. As soon as her toe touched it, a big pair of eyes opened.

Sasha jumped back and screamed.

The creature did the same.

"Wait a minute," said Sasha. "Hold on."

She stared directly at the grimy, filthy, little creature and still couldn't figure out where it ended and the dirt pile began.

"Are you trying to tell me something?"

The creature nodded. A cloud of soot bellowed outward.

It made a grunty noise like, "Ruh! Ruh!"

"Does 'ruh!' mean yes?" said Sasha.

"Ruh!"

"So why not just say yes then, if you

understand me?"

It shrugged.

"Well, are you a boy or a girl?" said Sasha.

Grunt.

"That wasn't a one-grunt or two-grunt question," said Sasha.

"Gooby gooby!" said the creature. Sasha didn't know what *gooby* meant, but there was no point in arguing with it. Sasha liked things to be clear and orderly. And she preferred people who bathed. Already, the palms of her hands felt like they needed a good washing, even though she hadn't touched the creature.

But even so, she had to admit, it was awfully cute. If she looked closely, it resembled a boy—about four years old—dressed in rags like the orphans of a castle

town in her books. He had tangled hair, and one grimy fist that seemed to be always in or near his mouth. His eyes were like giant puppy-dog eyes that expressed endless curiosity and kindness and just a little mischief.

Sasha watched him put a finger two knuckles deep into his nose.

"Well, you're very much like a pox," she said, "which is what my papa calls little unwanted things."

He nodded again. It was probably true.

"But if you weren't so dirty, you would remind me of the fairy folk, like Puck. Papa says Puck was luckier than a child in a storybook."

The little creature seemed to like that. He made a noise like a tiny walrus.

"Okay, we'll call you Puck."

"Ruh! Ruh!" said Puck, as though she had gotten the answer right.

He reached out two dirt-covered arms for a hug.

Sasha recoiled. “Look, Puck. You seem too silly and too messy for me to be friends with,” she said, “but it is nice to meet you.”

Puck let out a sound—a sad sound. A sound like his feelings had been hurt. He slumped back onto his dirt pile. His big black eyes started to water.

Sasha felt terrible and started to explain herself, but he simply tilted his head back, opened his mouth, and began to howl.

“Shh! What are you doing?!” said Sasha. “You’ll get us caught.”

But Puck didn’t seem to care that they were in an alley behind Ms. Kozlow’s shop. Sasha didn’t have any good excuse for hiding behind the chocolate shop. All she could do was admit that her papa had sold Ms. Kozlow a bunch of fake magic. Puck's howls grew even louder.

"Okay, okay, stop wailing. We'll be friends."

Puck wiped his tears with his arm, which made mud out of all the soot on his cheeks.

"You are a very difficult child…or dirt fairy… or whatever you are."

Puck snuffled up his tears and smiled.

"Now will you tell me whatever you were trying to tell me?" said Sasha. She was losing patience and daylight.

Ms. Kozlow had already had the potion for half an hour, and Sasha didn't have a clue why she needed it. Sasha could feel disaster in the air. And Puck seemed like nothing but a giant distraction.

"So?" said Sasha. "Will you tell me or not?"

Puck nodded at Sasha's hand.

Sasha looked down. She was still holding the chocolate bonbons Ms. Kozlow had given her.

"You have to be kidding me. You want this? That's what you were trying to say?" She held out the bonbons reluctantly.

In one quick motion, Puck opened his mouth and chomped on her whole hand.

"Ew!" said Sasha. She pulled her soggy hand away.

That was the second time Sasha had lost her bonbons. "Maybe you're not so lucky," she muttered—or maybe his luck was only for his own good.

Just then, Puck turned and scrambled up the gutter of Ms. Kozlow's shop.

"Hey!" said Sasha.

Puck climbed as fast as a squirrel and disappeared onto the roof and into the chimney.

Sasha sighed. "Of all the odds and oddity. What a disappointing creature," she said. All he'd wanted was the treat.

Sasha didn't have any friends, besides the possibility of Ms. Kozlow, which was a very exciting possibility. Sometimes she told herself it was because she was too busy. Her mother was gone, after all, and that left a lot of work for her to do. Besides, the kids all lived in the Village and went to school together. They all thought Sasha was the weird alchemist's daughter, who lived in the woods.

Still. It would have been nice, she thought, to have a partner.

Sasha was about to walk out of the alley, toward home, when she heard a scuffling sound at the window of the shop. The purple curtain flew away suddenly, and Puck's dirty face popped up behind the glass, smiling wide.

"Oh!" said Sasha, surprised and more than a little delighted.

Puck fumbled with the latch for a second, then pushed open the window. He waved for her to climb in.

"I thought you ran off," said Sasha.

"Pfft," said Puck, shaking his head at such a silly idea. "Gooby."

CHAPTER 5

Sasha was a detective and a scientist and the daughter of alchemists. She was a friend to dirt fairies (or whatever Puck was), and sometimes, she was a spy. But she was no thief and no sneakabout.

She didn't steal into people's homes, even if it would help the detecting and sciencing and spying.

"I won't do it," she said.

"Gooby!" said Puck, waving for her to hurry inside.

"No. Ms. K is an honorable woman. We won't betray her trust."

Puck let out a frustrated grunt.

He looked around the small back room of the shop where Ms. K had her pots, molds, and most importantly, the cooling racks for her macarons.

Sasha continued her speech. "Stealing of any kind is wrong, after all."

She looked up to see Puck already shoving three stolen macarons into his mouth.

"What are you doing? Stop that!"

He ate two more. She had no idea how he did it so fast.

"All right. If I come in, will you stop eating macarons?"

Puck shrugged.

"Fine. All right. I am obviously sneaking into this shop to stop you from committing any more crimes."

Sasha hoisted herself through the window just in time. The door to the back room opened. Light flooded in. Puck clamped his hand over Sasha's mouth and pushed her behind a giant gunnysack of cocoa powder.

He used his other hand to gesture *Shh*.

Sasha was more likely to scream about his dirty hand on her face than fear of any kind. It was Ms. Kozlow who had entered. She was speaking to someone in the showroom.

"...I keep them back here, since nobody ever asks for them. Hold on."

Ms. Kozlow seemed to grumble something to herself that Sasha couldn't hear. She pushed a few jars around. "Ah!" she said when she found the right one. She grabbed it and walked out.

Thankfully, she didn't close the door. Sasha

and Puck tiptoed out from behind the gunnysack to get a full view of the showroom.

Standing at the counter, leaning on the glass with one arm, and eyeing Ms. K with a cocky brow was a man named—

"Latouche is nothing if not prepared," said the man whose name must have been Latouche. Ms. K returned with the jar and placed it in front of him.

"Candy-coated almonds," she said.

"Ah. The perfect travel snack. How many different colors do you have?" he asked.

"Seven," said Ms. K.

"Oh? So few?" He laughed. Ms. Kozlow, who took her craft very seriously, did not laugh. Latouche coughed into his fist and stood up.

"Gooby," whispered Puck, shaking his head.

Latouche seemed to be about Ms. K's age. When he stood, he was tall, thin, and stiff, like stale taffy. He had a soldier's cap and black riding boots—and he was completely failing to charm.

He tried to gather himself by straightening an invisible mustache and saying, "Yes, well. This will do nicely. I'm traveling, you know."

"Yes, you mentioned," said Ms. Kozlow.

"Over the Sparkstone Mountains, past Rozny, all the way into the wilderlands. Only great adventurers do that."

"I hope you're packing more than almonds."

"I hope to bring a partner. A beautiful one."

"That's not very practical," said Ms. K.

"I mean, a partner for the adventure of life. A wife."

"And what about the adventure of the wilderlands?"

"Uh. Well. There's no exact date for departure. Latouche is nothing if not orderly. First, a wife. Second, pack the horse. Third, adventure! What do you say to all that? Can you help me with it?"

He smiled his charmingest smile and stepped back from the counter so she could get a good look at his handsomeness.

Ms. K handed him the jar and said, "I can help with the horse packing. Please let me know if you need any more, Sergeant."

It slowly dawned on Sergeant Latouche that this was not going the way he would have liked.

He straightened his posture and put the coins for the almonds on the counter.

"Very well," he said. "I may put off that adventure for now. My horse needs new shoes anyway. Maybe I'll build a house near the Willow Woods...or near the mountains. Maybe I'll buy Whispershaw Castle and clear out all the ghosts. Would you ever live in a castle? I only ask out of curiosity."

"Latouche is nothing if not curious," said Ms. K. "Have a very good day."

"Then off I go. Wish me luck!" said Latouche, as he bowed and turned to leave. Ms. K had sent him off, but she had been so kind that he left happily. Maybe she was secretly in love with Latouche? But then, why would she need luck from a potion? He obviously loved her back. Maybe the luck was to be rid of him? But he was easily the most handsome man in the Village.

As Latouche left the shop through the front door, Sasha climbed out the back window and ran down the alley. Puck stuffed another tray of macarons in his mouth and pockets and followed. “Hurry!” said Sasha. “We can’t lose him.”

Sasha dashed around the corner, hoping that Latouche was still in sight, when she ran smack into someone entering the chocolate shop and fell backward onto Puck.

CHAPTER 6

"Hey!" said Sisal Gentry.

Sasha had run right into Sisal and Basil Gentry.

"Of all the odds," she said to herself.

The Gentrys owned several farms around the Village, lots of shops, and even some of the Thistlewood—and Sisal, their young daughter, never let anyone forget it. She was Sasha's age, but that was all they had in common.

As Sasha picked herself up from the ground, Sisal shouted, "How dare you run into me! If you smudged my dress, you're paying for it. Help me up, Basil."

Basil was her older brother. Sasha thought it was the closest thing to magic that they were siblings. Where Sisal was narrow and cruel and loud, Basil was broad and modest and gentle.

He lifted her up and said, "Is everyone all right?"

"Everyone?" said Sisal. "Who cares if she's all right? Didn't you see her attack me? And what

is that next to you? Did you drag a dog through swamp mud?"

Puck growled at Sisal.

Sasha didn't have time for any of this. She looked up and down the cobblestone street, but there was no sign of Latouche.

"We lost him," she said.

"What have you lost, your mind?" said Sisal. "You still have to apologize to me."

With Latouche gone, Sasha returned to her present trouble. "I'm sorry, Sisal," she said.

"Well, 'sorry' isn't good enough."

"It will have to be good enough, Sissy," said Basil. "It was only an accident."

Sisal crossed her arms and gave a very practiced pout. "Then I want double the treats."

"Okay," said Basil. Then he turned to Sasha. "Sorry for the trouble."

"I'm not," said Sisal, as she stomped into the

chocolate shop.

"Quick," said Sasha when they had both entered the store. "Let's go back and listen. Maybe Ms. K wants luck to be rid of Sisal."

They hurried back into the alley and through the window once again. Puck grabbed another handful of macarons from the cooling trays as they snuck up to the back door.

Sisal was already flouncing around the shop, with Ms. K behind her. "This looks good," said Sisal. "Could I have a taste?"

Ms. K took a gooseberry bonbon and cut it into pieces. Sisal took two and popped them into her mouth.

"Mmm!" she said. "So good. Letty, you are my favorite new shopkeeper in town."

"Thank you," said Ms. K. "Should I put you down for some gooseberry then?"

"Not yet," said Sisal. "Can I try this one?"

Ms. K followed and reluctantly cut a rose caramel truffle for Sisal to try. And

then a lemon blossom, a maple tart, and a chocolate river stone. Each

time, Sisal raved and complimented Ms. Kozlow but never ordered any.

Finally, Basil said, “Sissy, I think we have enough information to make our decision.”

“But I want to try more,” said Sisal. “You never let me try anything.”

“Ms. Kozlow has been very kind to us, and patient.”

“You can call her Letty,” said Sisal.

“No. We don’t know Ms. Kozlow very well, so we give her the respect of calling her Ms. Kozlow until we know her better.” Then Basil cast a shy glance at Ms. Kozlow and said, “I think Sisal is saying in her own way that we would like to be your friends.”

Ms. Kozlow blushed.

Sasha whispered, "Could she be in love with Basil?"

She was a little older than he was, but not by much. And he was very kind. Sasha wondered if Ms. Kozlow would need luck to deal with his family. This case was starting to get complicated. "He obviously likes her," whispered Sasha, "but what do you think, Puck? Does she like him?"

Puck was spilling macaron crumbs everywhere as he devoured them. He nodded.

"No, I mean *like* like him."

He nodded again.

"Like in love with him."

Puck stopped and raised an eyebrow. He put another macaron in his mouth.

"Okay, maybe you're right. Then *why* does Ms. Kozlow need that blasted potion?"

Sasha was startled by the bell above the shop

door ringing as another customer entered the store. “It’s Gregor!” whispered Sasha.

Gregor Pavlov lived in a house on stilts in the middle of the Sweltering River with his elderly mother, nine pigeons, two cats, and an entire family of mice. The villagers said his father was an inventor. They said he had invented a walking house, even though no one had seen it walk. He had been called away, just like Sasha’s mom, to help the war effort.

From the looks of him, anyone could tell that Gregor wanted to be an inventor too. His clothes were disheveled, like he spent more time working in his lab than fixing himself up. He had machine oil smudged on his pants. His satchel was full of tools and mechanical oddities that fascinated Sasha. His brown hair was uncombed; his brown eyes were always wide open with curiosity.

He walked into the shop visibly nervous, perhaps because he too was afraid of the Gentrys buying up his father's house.

Sasha whispered to Puck, "You'll like Gregor. He's nice to kids...and nice to animals... whichever you are."

Puck ate more macarons and watched the show.

"Hi there, Letty," said Pavlov, fiddling with a clasp on his satchel.

"Hey! Wait your turn," said Sisal. "We were here first."

"I'm so sorry," said Basil. "Try this one, Sissy."

Gregor approached Ms. Kozlow. "I was hoping to get some more simple syrup...for my mice."

"Of course," said Ms. K. "How are they?"

"Very well. Thank you for watching them."

"Tell your mother I would be happy to do it again. They were no trouble."

"Wait," said Sisal, with half a bonbon still in her mouth. "Are you saying *your* hands touched a bunch of dirty mice and *then* made these bonbons? Gross! That's disgusting. I want a discount."

"You've eaten your discount," said Basil.

"I'm telling everybody," said Sisal.

"No, please. I was just away, and my mother couldn't watch them," said Gregor, trying to explain. "And the mice are very clean. Letty was very kind. She's a wonderful chocolatier."

"We agree," said Basil. "Don't we, Sissy?"

"I suppose. Can I try the ones on that top shelf?"

"Go ahead," said Ms. K. Sisal climbed up the stepladder to paw at the bonbons on the top shelf, and Ms. K took the moment to speak with Gregor as she gave him a small jar of syrup.

Gregor said, "I made you something to say

thanks." With shaking hands, he pulled a small mechanical rose from his satchel. "It's nothing. I made it with some scrap metal from my lab."

"I think she's going to cry," whispered Sasha.

"Oh, Gregor, that's so kind of you. Here, let me give you something in return." Ms. K reached under the counter and pulled out a particularly beautiful bonbon—the kind that was filled with cordial—and gave it to Gregor.

Gregor ate it immediately. His eyes went wide behind his glasses.

"It's a new flavor," said Ms. K.

"It's, um, good," said Gregor.

"It still needs work."

Gregor coughed loudly into his fist.

"Ew. Cover your mouth," said Sisal, even though he had covered his mouth.

"No, no. It's bold," said Gregor. "I think some people might like it."

Ms. K seemed embarrassed once again. Gregor tried to change the subject. "Have you visited Granny Yenta, yet?"

Ms. K winced at the mention of it.

For Sisal, it was like putting a cupcake in front of Otto; she dove right on it.

"Did you say, 'Granny Yenta'?"

"Stay out of it, Sissy."

"Are you going for a matchup? Is she going to find you a husband by asking her magical chicken? You are kind of pretty. Why can't you find your own boyfriend?"

"I think it's time we go," said Basil.

"I still have to try stuff," said Sisal.

"We'll take a box filled with everything she didn't try and a bill for everything she did," said Basil.

Ms. Kozlow began to put the box together.

"Fine," said Sisal. "But tell us why you're going at least."

Ms. Kozlow was a shade of red that Sasha had never seen before. She must have been mortified. "My father is making me go," she said finally.

"Ooh, but you're in love with someone else. I knew it!"

"That's her business," said Basil.

Gregor looked terribly sorry he had mentioned it.

"Come on, tell us! Is it a secret?"

Ms. Kozlow handed Basil the box and tried to smile, though she was obviously uncomfortable. "It's true," she said. "I have my own wishes for whom I'd like to marry. He's kind and smart, and I don't need Granny Yenta's matchmaking chicken to help me."

It was a sad situation.

"But is he handsome?" said Sisal.

Ms. Kozlow laughed. "Yes. Quite."

Basil dragged Sisal out of the shop. He bowed as they left, as if to apologize for her discomfort. Gregor dashed out just behind them. It was all too much awkwardness for anybody to handle.

"Did you hear all that?" Sasha whispered to Puck, who had eaten every last macaron on the cooling trays and was licking his fingers. "We've got our motivation—she needs luck for Granny Yenta's matchmaking services, and of all the odds, we've even got our suspects!"

“Okay,” said Sasha, pacing in front of the fountain in the Village center. “Get your finger out of your nose.”

Puck did not.

“Okay,” she said again. “We’ve got three potential suspects. All we have to do is figure out who Ms. Kozlow described as kind, smart, and handsome. Then we can give her the luck she needs. Get your finger out of your mouth.”

Puck did not.

Sasha kept pacing.

"Okay, let's see what we've got." She took out her detective notebook and wrote:

SUSPECTS across the top.

Sergeant Latouche. Wanted Ms. K to travel the world with him. Is handsome.

Basil Gentry. A little young but blushed every time he looked at her. Is very kind.

Gregor Pavlov. They seem to be friends already. Was sweating and nervous when he gave her rose. Is very smart.

Sasha looked over the notes. "Hmm. So Ms. Kozlow wants to marry one of these suspects, but if she leaves it to Granny Yenta, the odds aren't good. We have to find out who the lucky guy is."

Puck said, "Guh."

"What do you think, Puck? Should we start with Latouche? Get your foot out of your mouth."

Puck did not.

But that sparked an idea in Sasha. "You're right, Puck. Shoes! Latouche mentioned that his horse needed shoeing. We should go to the farrier to see if he's there. Don't look at me like that. *Farrier* means the person who puts shoes on horses. Don't shake your head. It does. What does that mean? Are you fluttering your arms like wings? What are you saying? No, farrier is not something more fairylike. Now what are you doing? Are you rowing a boat? No, I don't mean a person who ferries people across rivers. A farrier. Just trust me. We have to go."

So they went, but Puck still looked suspicious.

At the barn on the edge of the Village, Sasha pointed to a wooden sign that said: FARRIER, ONE SHOE, ONE GOLD. FOUR SHOES, FOUR GOLD. FIVE SHOES FOR THE PRICE OF FOUR.

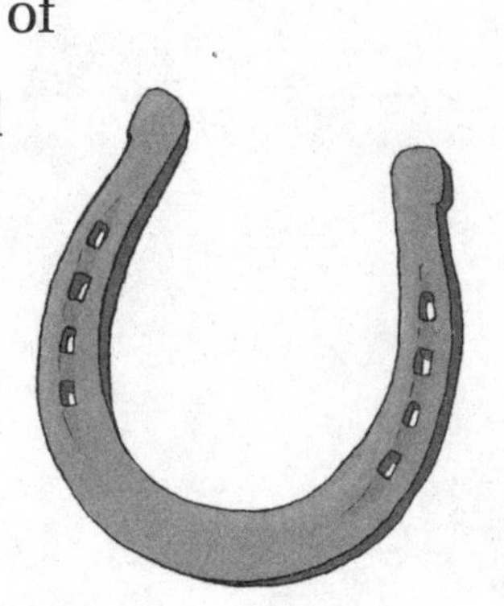

"See?" she said, "Farrier."

Puck shrugged.

Even before they turned the corner, they could hear Latouche. "Well, don't you have any, I don't know, snowshoes or something?"

He was standing by a horse that seemed too big for him, holding the reins a bit too tight. A bearded man in a worker's smock stood by—Sasha thought he was likely the farrier.

"Nope," he said. "This time of year, it's still too deep in the mountains for horses. Snow hasn't melted yet up there."

"Well, you're no help at all, are you?"

“Can’t melt the snow.”

Latouche wrenched the horse’s reins away and marched out of the barn. Sasha had to jump aside to make sure the creature didn’t knock her down. The old farrier stood by and kept chewing the straw in his mouth as if it didn’t bother him at all.

“He’s not very kind, is he?” said Sasha.

“Eh,” said the old man. “Probably for the best.

He'd get himself killed trying to ride that horse up a mountain."

The old man returned to his work. Sasha took out her notebook and wrote, *Not kind, and not very smart* under Latouche's name. "One down," she said. "Now, where do you think we'll find Basil?"

CHAPTER 8

The Gentry Mansion was all the way at the other end of Upside, where the first families lived. It was so big, it straddled over the Shivering River. The black stones arched over the water and jutted up into giant towers.

Sasha knew that somewhere in the world was the Citadel of the Make Mad Order—an evil place. She knew the Order of Disorder were the villains that her mother was fighting. But even in a world with the Citadel in it, she couldn't imagine a more frightening place than the Gentry Mansion.

"Remember what I told you," said Sasha as she and Puck walked along the tree-lined entranceway and approached the riveted oak door. "No biting, no stealing, no spitting."

Puck made a huffy noise.

Sasha thought about it as she lifted the metal knocker, shaped like a ring of thorns, and knocked. She quickly added, "You can bite in self-defense. I don't mind if you steal Sisal's chocolate, and if they say something truly awful and you need to spit, then go ahead, but try not to."

Puck was much happier with that arrangement. The oak door swung heavy on its hinges. In the doorway stood Vadim Gentry, master of the mansion. Sasha and Puck both had to crane their necks to look up at him. He was so tall, his head almost touched the top of the doorway. He was so broad, his shoulders almost touched the sides of the doorway.

Sasha had not thought Vadim himself would open the door. It would usually be their butler, or maid, or horseman. She never would have knocked if she'd known. He spoke with a deep, unhappy voice, and did not say hello.

"I was taking my wife for her walk."

"Um. Very sorry to bother you, Mr. Gentry."

"You're the Bebbin girl."

"Yes. We're here to see Basil. Is he around?"

"How's your father's business doing?"

"Oh, very good," said Sasha. "If you ever need potions or medicine, we'd be happy to help." Sasha didn't want Vadim Gentry to think he could buy their store anytime soon. He always seemed to be waiting for his opportunity. Vadim stepped back into the house and pushed forward a chair with wheels that Sasha knew had been made by Gregor's father.

In the chair sat Rose Gentry with a blanket on her lap. She was as white as paper, with long brown hair that reminded Sasha of Basil. "Hello," said Mrs. Gentry. Her smile was so warm and wilted and gentle. Sasha knew that she had been sick a long time.

"Hi, Mrs. Gentry," said Sasha. "I was just telling Mr. Gentry that if you ever need anything for your headaches..."

Mrs. Gentry laughed weakly. "Oh, I know, dearest. Your mother was a great help to me. Have you heard from her?"

"Not recently," said Sasha.

Mrs. Gentry seemed like the kind of woman Sasha's mother would like. She took a box out from under the blanket on her lap and said, "My children bought me some bonbons. May I offer you some? Go on. You can take one."

Puck jumped forward and took two, which made Mrs. Gentry laugh. He ate them immediately. Sasha took a peanut butter chew as she glared at Puck and put it in her satchel for later.

"Thank you," she said. "That's very kind of you."

Vadim pushed the chair, so there wasn't much time to discuss Sasha's mother. "I miss her very much," said Rose.

But Sasha didn't have a chance to say, *Me too.*

Over his shoulder, Vadim said, "Basil's in the gardens, around the back. Beware of Abrus. He's off his leash and will happily eat your friend."

"Well," said Sasha, as they watched Vadim walk Rose along the courtyard. "That was intense."

"Guh," said Puck.

"I know," said Sasha. "He's always like that."

As they walked around the Gentry Mansion, Sasha said, “Abrus is their dog.”

“Eh,” said Puck. He seemed to be unfazed. If he lived on the streets, he probably had to deal with dogs all the time. “Well, even so,” said Sasha, “if he comes for you, forget everything I said about biting and spitting, okay?”

Puck nodded and punched his hand, like he was ready for a fight…which was kinda funny, ’cause he had the cutest chubby cheeks Sasha had ever seen.

They turned the corner onto a stone patio with an arched row of columns. At the foot of each column was a star-shaped flower bed full of perfectly straight, black tulips. Beyond the black tulip portico was a grove of olive trees where they could see Basil and Sisal playing with a dog so big, it could have been a bear.

"Maybe we shouldn't have come," said Sasha.

"Hey!" said Sisal. "What are you doing here?"

As soon as Abrus saw them, he barked, but Basil held him around the neck.

"No, Abrus!" said Basil.

"What are you doing here?" demanded Sisal.

Sasha realized she had no reason to give them, besides her secret mission. "Uh," she said, "we just came to say sorry for bumping into you at the chocolate shop."

"You came all the way up here for that?"

"Yes," said Sasha. She grabbed Puck's hand and began to walk back around the house. Sisal narrowed her eyes. "You're weird, Sasha Bebbin, and I don't like you."

Sasha's detective skills were failing her. She

didn't have a plan. "Okay, well, I was also hoping to see if Basil was interested in joining a science expedition I'm leading into the Willow Woods...to study...meadow flowers."

"What? That's ridiculous," said Sisal. "You can't speak with him. He's my brother."

"He's standing right here."

"I don't care."

Sasha looked at Basil, who shrugged.

Meanwhile, Puck was tense and staring at Abrus. This gave Sasha an idea. "How about this?" she said. "If Puck can race Abrus and win, you let me talk to your brother."

"That thing? Race my Abrus? Are you joking?"

"Puck will win," said Sasha with a smirk. Puck nodded.

"Fine," said Sisal. She leaned back and hurled her ball as far as she could. "Go, Abrus! Fetch!"

The dog-bear took off. Puck stood still.

He looked up at Sasha with a questioning look.

"Go," said Sasha.

As quick as a pixie, he leapt into action. Abrus was fast, but Puck was a blur. He raced under the ball before it even hit the ground, caught it in his mouth, and ran back. Abrus gave chase.

Puck zipped up to Sasha and gave her the wet ball.

"See?" said Sasha. But her comment was cut short. Abrus was still running at them. And he looked furious. Sasha didn't even have time to scream before Puck jumped in front of her. She could hear his tiny growl as he stood his ground in front of the beast that was ten times his size.

Sasha had to think quickly.

She reached into her satchel and grabbed the peanut butter chew she'd gotten from Mrs. Gentry. Then she threw it right at Abrus. The dog jumped

in the air and caught it and became distracted with the gooey peanut butter in its mouth.

That was the third time in one day that Sasha had lost her dessert.

Puck was still growling. Sasha approached and touched him on the shoulder.

"It's okay, Puck. You did it."

Puck was shaking. As soon as she touched him, he turned around and hugged Sasha's legs.

"It's okay," she said.

"Gooby," he said, still shaken up. "Gooby gooby."

Basil ran up to Abrus and put the leash back on him. "I'm sorry," he said.

"Who cares? Is Abrus okay?" said Sisal. "If your dirty, little rat creature had attacked him, my dad would have ruined you."

"It was your dog's fault," said Sasha. "He lost the race. Puck was just protecting me."

"There's no need to threaten them, Sissy," said Basil.

"Why not? They're on our land."

"That makes them our guests."

"Ugh. Basil. Papa's right about you. You can be soft in the heart or soft in the head, but you can't be both."

Sasha could see that this cut Basil deeply. Even Sisal seemed to realize she'd gone too far.

"We'll go," said Sasha.

"Thanks anyway," said Basil. "I wouldn't be any good on a science expedition."

They ran back around the mansion, along the walkway in front, over the little bridge across the Shivering River, and back down the hill toward the Village.

"That was probably a mistake," said Sasha.

"Guh," said Puck.

"But did you notice what she said?"

“Guh,” said Puck.

“No, not the part about you being a dirty rat creature. I’m sorry about that. It was hurtful, but you must admit you need a bath. But anyway, not that. The part about Basil. It was awfully mean.”

“Guh. Guh.”

“Okay, both comments were mean. But the one about Basil was about being kind or dumb. I don’t think Basil is dumb, but he must be struggling

with his schooling. That's why it hurt him. He must think she's telling the truth."

Sasha got out her notebook and wrote a note under Basil's name: *Handsome and kind but not smart.*

Then she felt bad and changed it to: *...not exactly the smartest, but still a good person with other wonderful qualities.*

Either way, she thought, they had their solution. It was Gregor that Ms. Kozlow loved. He was kind to his mice and passionate about his lab, certainly. Maybe Ms. Kozlow thought that made him handsome as well. The sun was starting to set, and Ms. K would be going to Granny Yenta soon. Sasha started to run again.

"We have to find Gregor, or we're sunk."

They couldn't find him.

"Of all the odds and oddity!" said Sasha. They had searched all over the Village, but Gregor Pavlov was nowhere to be found.

The sun had set, and the last remains of twilight were beginning to fade. Papa would be wondering where she was. But Sasha wouldn't give up.

"We've cracked the case, Puck, and we're still lost."

"Guh."

They walked to Ms. Kozlow's shop. At the

very least, they could try to give her a little encouragement that her luck would pick up the next day. They crossed the bridge into Upside and approached Le Bon Bonbon. Even at a distance, they could see the lights of the shop were dark.

"Uh oh," said Sasha.

"Uh oh," repeated Puck.

The door of the shop suddenly opened, and Ms. K walked out, wearing a bright-yellow dress, mud boots, and her blue traveling hood. She locked the door and turned the wooden sign to the side that said "Closed for Business."

"She must be going to Granny Yenta tonight!" said Sasha. "Quick, Puck, I have a mission for you."

Puck straightened up and made a salute.

"Run back to my house and get a bag of special hazelnut oatmeal feed from the chicken coop, then meet me at Granny Yenta's."

Puck was off at a full run on all fours before she could finish. "And don't eat it all," she shouted after him.

Then she turned and ran the other direction after Ms. Kozlow.

"Hi, Ms. K. What are the odds I'd bump into you here?"

"We're in front of my shop," said Ms. K, a bit confused.

"Ha! I guess the odds are pretty good then."

Sasha made sure not to ask permission to walk with Ms. K, because she wouldn't have gotten it. Ms. Kozlow seemed even more nervous than she had been back at Papa's shop.

"If you'll excuse me," she said, "I do have an appointment."

"I'll go with you," said Sasha. "Friends stick together."

Ms. K smiled and wiped a happy tear from

her cheek. It occurred to Sasha how difficult it would be to move to a new village to start a new shop with no one else but a father who seemed to be very strict. Maybe Sasha was Ms. Kozlow's only friend, the same way that she was Sasha's.

"Thank you," said Ms. Kozlow.

"It's lucky to find a friend in a world as big as ours, isn't it?"

Ms. Kozlow nodded.

They walked downriver, through the cheap market, where everyone was closing up for the night. The lamplighter tipped her hat to them as she held her metal rod up to a streetlight. A warm glow radiated from the lamp.

Before they reached Dockside, they turned and left the Village on a small stone path that led into Thistlewood Swamp, the wetlands between the sea and the Willow Woods.

The path narrowed as they passed thistles

and crags, until it was just a line of stones surrounded by mud. They walked single file as they balanced on the rocks.

Most of the time, they walked in silence toward Granny Yenta's hut, which was deep in the swamp, in a glade of gnarled trees that looked like unhappy spirits. Everything in the swamp seemed to be thorny and poisonous. It was dark, but they could see the torches lit up around Granny Yenta's cottage.

Anyone who could survive there must be a tough person. “Do you think you’ll get what you want?” said Sasha as they began to approach the stone cottage.

“I hope so,” said Ms. K. She seemed to be thinking about more things than she could carry. Then she said, “You have a nice dad.”

"Thanks," said Sasha. She wanted to be more helpful. "And he's very good. I'm sure you'll have the luck you need."

Ms. K smiled as she used the stone mallet to knock on the metal door of the cottage. "I have a good feeling that you're right," she said. "In fact, I—"

Before she could finish, they heard a "Heads up!" from inside the small cottage. The door swung open, and Granny Yenta flung a bucket of water all over Ms. Kozlow.

"Ooh," said Sasha, wincing at the sight of Ms. Kozlow soaked from head to toe. "That's unlucky."

CHAPTER 10

Granny Yenta was not a witch, but people said she had some goblin in her, and that's why she had a greenish complexion. She was not tall, and she was not safe. But she was not false, and she was not weak.

"Ack! I'm so sorry," she said. "You must be Letty Kozlow. The version of you that has fallen into a lake, I mean."

Granny Yenta didn't invite them inside her cottage. Instead, she walked out, grabbed Ms. K by the hand, and walked her around the house.

"Come with me to the back. We'll perform the ceremony there."

Ms. Kozlow was still shivering from the shock of being doused with freezing cold well water.

"Was soaking her part of the ceremony?" said Sasha, rushing to keep up with them.

"What? Who's this? Who're you?"

"I'm Sasha Bebbin."

"Maxima's daughter?"

"That's my mom."

"I liked her. How is she?"

"Still gone. Is this supposed to be a magic ceremony?"

"Oh. Sorry, kid."

"Do you hit her with water and wait to see which of the boys gets a cold or something?"

"What? No. Nothing that silly," said Granny Yenta, waving away the silliness. She led them around the stone house to a sparse dirt lot, where a particularly arrogant rooster was walking in circles, waiting for dinner.

"Are you going to use the chicken?" said Sasha. "I thought you'd use the chicken to detect her heart vibrations or something."

Granny Yenta stopped and looked at Sasha for the first time. She lifted her glasses to squint at her, then squinted at her through the glasses some more. "You are an odd little child," she said.

"So I'm right about the chicken," said Sasha.

"He's a rooster. His name is Samson, and he doesn't *detect her vibrations*." She said that last part in a namby-pamby voice. "He's magic."

Granny explained that in the pen next to the chicken, she had poured chicken feed on the ground in the shape of every letter of the alphabet. When she let Samson into the yard, he would peck at the letters and spell out the name of Ms. Kozlow's future husband.

"Right, okay," said Sasha. "So then why soak her with water?"

"That was just an accident," said Granny Yenta. "I was gonna mop my floor, and there was a spider in there."

Then she turned to Ms. K and said, "Sorry about that, dear."

"It's no trouble," said Ms. K. She'd become a bit sheepish, either because she'd just heard that Granny had thrown a spider on her, or because her entire fate depended on a magical chicken. "Granny Yenta," she pleaded, "would it be possible to ask your chicken my future? I would love to make this quick and quiet."

Unfortunately for Ms. K, that was when they heard the hubbub of people walking around the cottage to the dirt lot.

"Of all the odds," said Sasha.

"Sorry, dear," said Granny Yenta, "but we've got company."

"Blast my luck," said Ms. K.

Latouche, Basil, Sisal, Gregor, and Papa all emerged from around the house in various forms of panic.

"I've come to save the day!" said Latouche, panting.

"We thought you were in trouble," said Basil.

"Why?" said Ms. K. She looked horrified that everyone would be there to see her match-making ceremony.

"There was a sign on your shop door," said Gregor. "It said LOVE EMERGENCY in a hasty scrawl. It looked like someone had used coal dust, and it was misspelled. We thought you were in danger."

Granny Yenta scoffed at the idea.

"Right," said Latouche, "except the sign said SAVE ME, LATOUCHE."

Sisal chimed in, "I thought it said NO MORE CHOCOLATE."

Papa said, "To me, the sign looked like it said HELP SASHA, so I came running."

"How could the same sign say such different things?" said Sasha.

"It was really bad handwriting," said Papa.

"Okay, enough," said Granny Yenta. "Time for everyone to go."

The crowd erupted into everyone talking at once. In the chaos, Sasha felt a pull on her sleeve. She looked down to see Puck beside her.

"Was this your doing?" said Sasha. "I didn't even know you could write."

Puck shrugged and held out the bag of hazelnut feed. Sasha noticed he had bruises on his arms, a few new scratches on his cheek, and it was hard to tell—his hair being so messy to begin with—but clumps of it were missing.

"What happened to you? Did you get in a fight with Otto? Our pig Otto?"

Puck tensed and growled when she said Otto's name. Sasha felt a pang of guilt for sending him unaware into such a dangerous situation. But there was no time for that now.

"Quick," she said, "keep them distracted."

The group was still arguing about what the sign said, what it meant, and whether or not they were needed at the matchmaking.

Sasha squeezed between the fence posts and quickly poured the hazelnut feed over some of the letters. It was the special blend that Papa had made when their chickens got sick. They loved it. She hoped Samson would too.

"Hurry! Hurry!" she said to herself. The chatter was starting to fade, and someone would notice her soon. Just then, Samson let out a terrible screech, fluttered his wings, and flew into Granny Yenta's arms. Everyone turned to look.

Sasha was the only one to notice the shadow of Puck disappearing behind the chicken coop. In his mouth was a bunch of Samson's tail feathers.

Sasha finished pouring the feed and dashed out of the lot. She joined the group and did her best to look like she'd been there the whole time.

"All right, all right," said Granny Yenta. "You bunch of milk drinkers can stay. But don't touch anything or say anything or get in the way. And don't sigh if you don't get what you want. And don't stand around my house crying or anything. We do the thing, she gets her match, then you leave. Ten minutes after, I'll set my slime buzzards loose, and you don't want to be around when they're hungry."

Everyone agreed. They stood a little closer to each other, out of a new fear for slime buzzards.

Granny carried Samson to the lot. She whispered gentle words to him, then she put him down. They all stood by the fence to see where he would go.

Sasha hoped her plan was enough. It was a logical method. But would it work? Did Samson work by logic, or did he have supernatural matchmaking pecks that worked only by magic?

She didn't know.

Samson took a few steps into the lot and began to peck at a particular mound of feed.

"L," said Granny Yenta.

"That's the last letter in *Basil*!" shouted Sisal, even though *L* was the first letter in Latouche's name. She was probably imagining herself getting endless boxes of chocolate.

"Shh," said Basil, though he was already red in the cheeks.

The rooster walked to another mound and pecked at it.

"A," said Granny. "O."

"Latouche," said Latouche with a triumphant smirk. "I knew she was in love with me. I'll admit, Latouche is nothing if not a little lonely."

Everyone watched Samson, hoping he would peck some more. Latouche continued, "Mrs. Latouche…wait, what's your first name?"

Ms. Kozlow had her head in her hands. "Leticia," she said from behind her fingers.

"Leticia Latouche," said Latouche. It didn't really have a ring to it.

Sasha was beginning to worry. All day, Ms. Kozlow had had the worst luck imaginable. Surely she would blame Papa, and Papa would go out of business, and the Gentrys would buy the shop and kick them out.

"V," said Granny Yenta. Then, "P. Looks like we have our winner."

Everyone turned to Gregor Pavlov, whose eyes had been closed the entire time. He opened them. They were full of a kind of joy that Sasha could only describe as supernatural. He laughed. Ms. Kozlow was crying. "I was hoping it would be you," she said.

"Oh, Letty," said Gregor. "You've made me the luckiest man in the world."

They ran into each other's arms.

Everyone clapped, even Latouche and Basil, because, at the end of the day, all of them were on the side of true love.

Sasha laughed. She heard a "woop!" next to her and saw that Puck had reappeared beside her.

He stuffed a fistful of hazelnut feed into his mouth and gobbed on the paste it made.

Letty and Gregor kissed twice.

Then Granny Yenta walked to the buzzard cages, and the crowd had to disperse. As they marched out of Thistlewood Swamp, Ms. K shook Papa's hand. "Thank you," she said. "You saved me."

She kissed Papa on the cheek.

Sasha ran up to walk next to them. "Seems like the potion worked, huh? You had great luck after all."

Ms. K laughed. "Oh. It wasn't me. I had

terrible luck today. Look at me. I'm soaked." She slipped her arm around Gregor's and said, "But Mr. Pavlov, on the other hand..."

Gregor's eyes went wide. "You mean...was there a potion in that bonbon you gave me?"

Ms. K smiled and put her head on his shoulder. "I know you don't believe in them," she said.

"I believe in you," he said, holding her close. "But no wonder it tasted so foul."

"I told her to mix jam with it," said Papa.

"So Gregor was the lucky one," said Sasha. She looked at Puck. "We knew that."

Puck nodded.

CHAPTER 13

Granny Yenta had escorted them through the swamp and into the Village. At first, Sasha thought it was to protect them from her buzzards. But then they reached the Village, and she kept walking. Maybe she had some business at the night market.

Sasha watched as she said to Papa, "Mr. Bebbin, I am impressed with your potionography."

"Thank you, Granny," said Papa.

"I think we could do some business," she said.

"Oh? Is there something I can help you with?"

Granny Yenta looked around, to make sure no one else could hear. Then she whispered something into Papa's ear. Sasha tried to scoot up to hear, but she missed it.

Whatever it was, it meant she'd have another mission soon.

Papa shook Granny's hand and said, "I'll have it for you in the morning."

It was a fresh spring evening. Everything was flowering, and the streetlamps were all aglow.

At the Village center, everyone went their own way. Basil and Sisal called the coachman to drive them to Upside. Gregor and Ms. K walked arm in arm toward her shop. Sergeant Latouche

wandered toward the inn.

That left Sasha, Papa, and Puck.

"It was really nice to meet you," said Sasha.

"Guh!" said Puck.

"I suppose I'll see you around?"

"Guh! Guh!"

"I think we should probably become friends."

Puck nodded so vigorously that his whole body seemed to bounce. He reached into a tattered pocket and pulled out a macaron from Ms. Kozlow's shop. It was completely smashed, and his hands were covered in dirt, but he held it out to Sasha with eyes as wide and hopeful as a puppy's.

"You want me to eat that?" said Sasha.

Puck nodded.

Sasha thought about all the desserts she had lost that day and all the terrible luck. And yet she had made a friend, and even though he was dirty and made her nose wrinkle up, he had been thinking of her. Sasha popped the macaron into her mouth. It was delicious.

Puck clapped his hands as she chewed it.

“Thank you,” she said. She expected him to break off, but he walked with them all the way through Downside and out of the Village, toward their home. Sasha was suddenly struck with the question: Where did Puck live, exactly?

Papa walked beside her and said, “Would your friend like to spend the night? I bet we could find a rug or something, or maybe a box full of straw.”

Puck clapped and howled and hugged Papa’s leg all the way up the hill.

Sasha did the same.

“You know,” said Papa, “I smelled the fumes from that luck potion and had wonderful things happen to me all day. I even got a new customer with Granny Yenta.”

"Well, I smelled the fumes and had horrible luck all day," said Sasha.

Papa put his arm around her shoulders. She loved it when he did that.

He said, "It seems to me you had a magical day. You saved Letty Kozlow. You helped Gregor find a wife ten times his better. And you made a new friend."

"I even got dessert out of it," admitted Sasha.

They both laughed.

However it had happened, Sasha and Puck had done it. They'd saved the day…or at least made sure nothing horrible had happened. The new couple was awfully in love. Papa's shop had kept its reputation for magical abilities, and, maybe luckiest of all, Sasha and Puck had found each other.

100 Years of Albert Whitman & Company

1919–2019

Present — Albert Whitman & Company encompasses all ages and reading levels, including board books, picture books, early readers, chapter books, middle grade, and YA

2017 — *The Boxcar Children* celebrates i
75th anniversary and the secon
Boxcar Children movie, *Surpri*
Island, is scheduled to be releas

2014 — The first Boxcar Children movie is released

2008 — John Quattrocchi and employe
Pat McPartland buy Albert
Whitman & Company, continui
the tradition of keeping it
independently owned and opera

1989 — *Losing Uncle Tim*, a book about the AIDS crisis, wins the first-ever Lambda Literary Award in the Children's/YA category

1970 — The first Albert Whitman
issues book, *How Do I Feel?* b
Norma Simon, is published

1956 — Three states boycott the company after it publishes *Fun for Chris*, a book about integration

1942 — *The Boxcar Children* is published

1938 — *Pecos Bill: The Greatest Cowboy of All Time* wins a Newbery Honor Award

1919 — Albert Whitman & Company
is started

Early 1900s — Albert Whitman begins his career in publishing